Animal Friends
for
Bedtime

Storybook Collection

This book belongs to:

....

A catalogue record for this book is available from the British Library

Published by Ladybird Books Ltd
27 Wrights Lane London W8 5TZ
A Penguin Company
2 4 6 8 10 9 7 5 3 1

Stories in this book were previously published by Ladybird Books Ltd.
in the *Picture Ladybird* series.
Who am I? ©text/illustrations Ladybird Books
Jasper's Jungle Journey ©text/illustrations Val Biro
The Star that Fell ©text Karen Hayles ©illustrations Cliff Wright
This Way Little Badger ©text Phil McMylor ©illustrations Cliff Wright
The Great Rabbit Race ©text/illustrations Ladybird Books

Animal Friends
for
Bedtime

Storybook Collection

Ladybird

Contents

The Star that Fell

by Karen Hayles
illustrated by Cliff Wright

The Great Rabbit Race

by Geraldine Taylor
illustrated by Lesley Smith

This way Little Badger

by Phil McMylor
illustrated by Cliff Wright

Who am I?

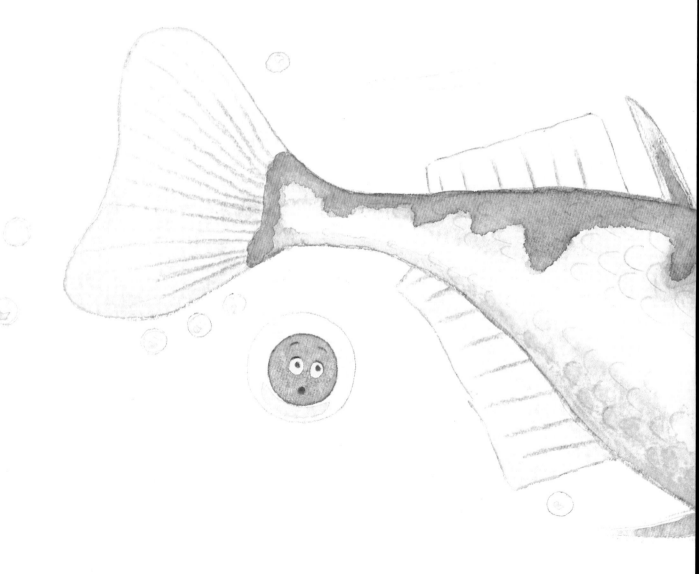

George was sad.

He couldn't jump, he couldn't jiggle.

He couldn't run, he couldn't wriggle.

All he could do was...

dream,

drifting by the weeds

in the dark, dark pond.

"Who am I?" he asked the water-boatman.

The water-boatman was far too busy to stop.

He stared crossly.

"Who are you?
You're a dot,
you're a spot,
you're a jelly-belly tot.
You're an inky-pinky blot
in the dark, dark pond!"

The water-boatman kicked his legs proudly,
and darted away through
the weedy water.

George was sad.

He couldn't dart,

he couldn't hop.

He couldn't start,

he couldn't stop.

All he could do was dream,

drifting by the weeds

in the dark, dark pond.

"Who am I?"

he asked the stickleback.

The stickleback wriggled closer,

then she giggled.

"Who are you?
You're a dot,
you're a spot,
you're a jelly-belly tot.
You're an inky-pinky blot
in the dark, dark pond!"

The stickleback flicked her tail proudly,
and danced away through
the weedy water.

George waited sadly.
He couldn't dance,
he couldn't kick.
He couldn't glide,
he couldn't flick.

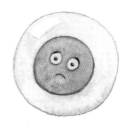

But each day he grew just
a little bigger...

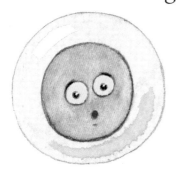

and bigger...
and bigger...

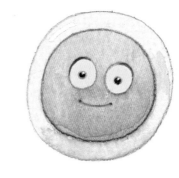

One day the stickleback wriggled past again.

"Fiddle-my-fins,
Fiddle-my-fins—
you're getting fat!
And fiddle-my-
fiddledy-diddledy-fins—
just what do you think
is THAT?"

George looked behind
to find a...

TAIL!

He waved it, he wiggled it.

He flicked it, he jiggled it.

"Now who am I?" he asked in excitement.

"Pooh! I've already told you that,"

said the stickleback, rudely.

"You're a dot,
you're a spot,
you're a jelly-belly tot.
You're an inky-pinky blot
in the dark, dark pond!"

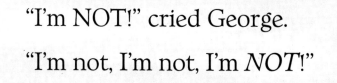

"I'm NOT!" cried George.

"I'm not, I'm not, I'm *NOT!*"

And this time,

to his surprise,

he darted forward.

The stickleback

wriggled off in alarm.

Each day George grew bigger...

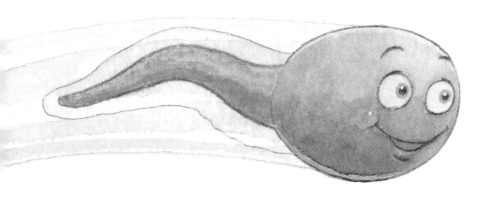

and bigger...

and bigger...

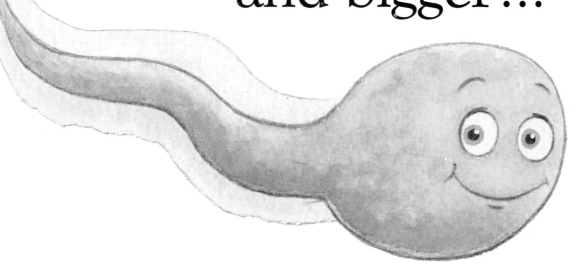

One day the water-boatman darted by again.

When he saw George this time

he stopped and stared.

He looked puzzled.

"What's this?
You're not a dot
or a spot!
You're not a jelly-belly tot
any longer."

George looked behind
to find...

LEGS!

He looked, he kicked,
he licked his lips.

The water-boatman darted off in alarm,
and George kicked again.

He landed rather breathlessly
on a slithery, sunny rock by the edge
of the dark, dark pond.
He stared around. Then he smiled
and blinked happily.

"I can do it!"

"I can dance, I can kick,
I can glide, I can flick!

I can jump, I can jiggle,
I can race, I can wriggle!

I can swim, I can hop,
I can jelly-belly flop!

I can leap to a leaf,
I can dive to a log!

I can slide, I can hide,
I am ME!   I am…

FROG!"

Jasper's
Jungle Journey

Jasper the little elephant had lost his
teddy bear in the jungle.

First, he searched the tall green grass.
What did he see?

A snake in coils, bright as brass!

Then, behind a twisted tree,
what did he see?

Two chimps having chips and tea!

By some rough and rugged rocks,
what did he see?

A lion, wearing purple socks!

On the bank of a reedy river,
what did he see?

A croc with a cold, all a-shiver!

In the swampy slushy ooze,
what did he see?

A hippo yawn, before his snooze!

Jasper on his search for bear,
what did he see?

A giraffe without a care!

By some trees all tossed and torn,
what did he see?

A rhino with an enormous horn!

In a stripey-shaded nook,
what did he see?

A zebra, reading a cookery book!

Searching for bear under the trees,
what did he see?

A camel wearing dungarees!

Then he got a fearful fright,
what did he see?

A roaring tiger. What a sight!

Jasper ran home. And when he got there,
what did he see?

Mum – who had found his teddy bear!

The Star
that Fell

One night a star fell...

Fox found the star first...

and she took it back to her den so that
her cubs would feel safe in the dark.

Badger noticed the glow…

and he borrowed the star to light his
way through the inky wood.

Owl came across the star and
she flew it to a tall tree so that
she could see it from afar.

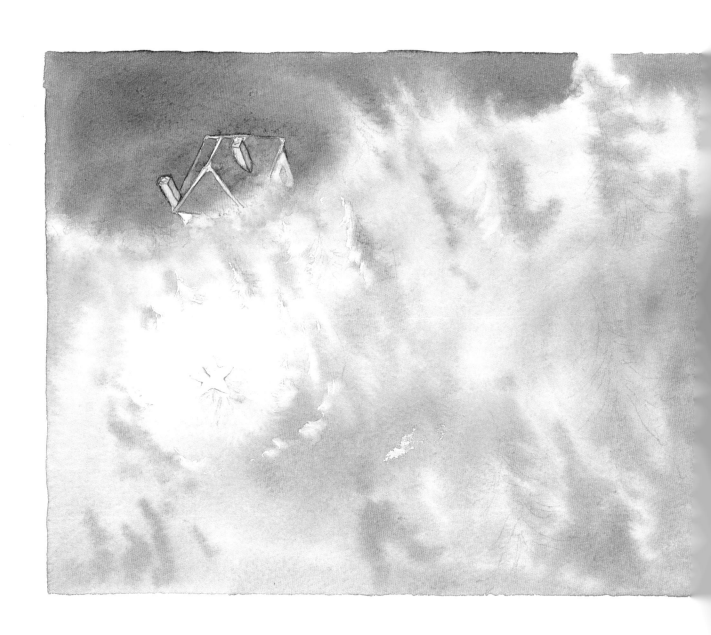

When Squirrel woke the next morning…

she took her children to see the
wonderful star that Owl had put
at the top of their tree.

Magpie stole the bright star…

and he hid it in his nest with all the
other glittering things.

Stag knocked the star from the nest…

Rabbit found it soon afterwards.
She carried it back to her warren to
keep her babies warm.

Dog dug up the star…

and he gave it to his friend
Maddy as a gift.

Maddy ran home with the star…

and she put it in her secret box of
very special things.

But the star began to fade.

Maddy's father said the star belonged
to the sky and they must give it back.

So that night Maddy opened her bedroom window and set the star free. Up… up… it zoomed into the dark sky, growing brighter and brighter as it went.

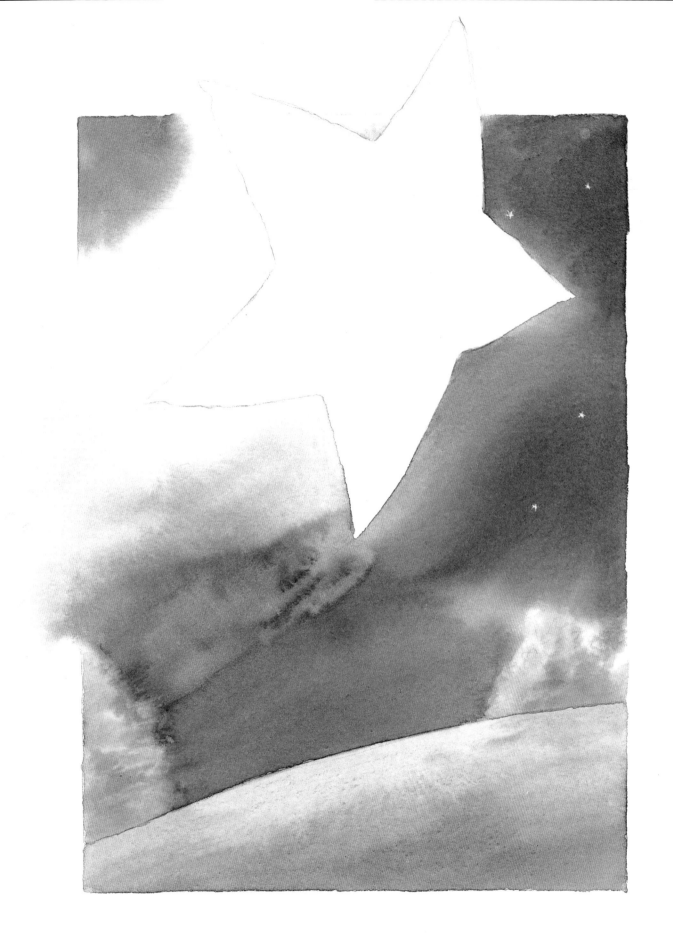

Now every evening before she goes to sleep,
if the sky is clear and she looks very carefully,
Maddy can see her star twinkling
in its place amongst all the others...
just where it always was.

The Great
Rabbit Race

"I want to see what's *outside*," said the little brown rabbit; "we've been up and down every tunnel in this warren. Let's go *outside*..." He crept towards the bright light and two other little brown rabbits followed. Their little grey sister held back. She remembered that their mother had warned them never, *absolutely never*, to go outside without her...

Suddenly their mother appeared, large and cross.

"Listen to me, little rabbits. Outside is a big, thrilling place – but it's dangerous and you must obey the rules. *Never* go outside alone – not until you've earned your grown-up names."

Little grey rabbit twitched her ears in excitement and wondered what *her* grown-up name would be.

"There's a lot to learn first," said her mother. "Line up, don't dawdle, follow me – we're going outside."

On the warm grass outside the warren, Mother Rabbit watched her little rabbits race each other up and down the bank, their white tails bobbing. Then she taught them to sniff the air, to sit up on their back legs to look around – and to listen with their long ears for the faintest sounds from far away.

"And if you hear *this* noise, little rabbits," she said, "there's *danger* outside and you must race home as fast as you can." She lifted one of her long back feet and hit the ground with a loud, hollow thump.

"Now," she said, "say your rabbit drill –
Sniff and listen,
Look around,
If there's danger, thump the ground.
Then run, rabbits, RUN..."

Free to explore while her mother watched, little grey rabbit gave two excited jumps for joy, dashed in circles and tumbled down the bank. Her three brothers raced after her and then all four rabbits stopped as still as stones, sat up and peeped into a huge black hole.

"That," said little grey rabbit, "is an *enormous* rabbit hole."

"*Giant* rabbits live there," said one of her brothers. "Look – something's coming – it's…"

But no one could hear him. A long, shining and deafening creature shot out of the giant hole and roared along a gleaming path. The three brown rabbits were frozen with fear, but little grey rabbit turned and ran like the wind back to her mother.

"I've seen danger! Danger's down there!" she cried.

"Little rabbits," said their mother, "that's a *train*. Keep well away. But it's not the train you've to run from. It's the red shape watching the train. That's the *fox*. Always run from the fox."

"I smelt the fox!" said one of the little brown rabbits. "It was *horrible*."

"That's true," said his mother. "Your grown-up name is Sharp Nose. You will warn us about foxes."

Four little rabbits danced in the sunlight while
far away, and hidden, the fox sat watching.

That night, their mother led the little rabbits outside again and they tiptoed cautiously into the darkness.

As little grey rabbit looked up at the sky, black clouds parted and an enormous white face frowned down at her.

She ran like the wind to her mother.

"I've seen danger! Danger's up there!"

"Little rabbits," said their mother, "That's the *moon*. It's not the moon you've to run from. It's the dark wings that cross the moon. That's the *owl*. Always hide from the owl."

"I heard the owl crying," said one of the little brown rabbits.

"That's true," said his mother. "Owls cry in the night. Your grown-up name is Sharp Ears. You will warn us about owls."

"And I saw something move in the woods..." said his brother. "It was black and white..."

"That was a *badger*," said his mother. "Badgers wear the colours of moonlight. Never trust badgers. Your grown-up name, little rabbit, is Sharp Eyes. You will warn us about badgers."

Little grey rabbit felt silly. She had been running too fast to hear the owl or see the badger – but she wanted her grown-up name, too.

Four little rabbits stared at the stars while far away, and hidden, the fox sat watching.

One morning, as the stars faded and the clouds turned pink, the little rabbits raced, and practised their rabbit drill. Then, while their mother watched, they crept close to the giant train tunnel, where the grass and dandelions grew thickly.

Suddenly, the ground shook and an enormous train roared from the tunnel.

As it thundered along, little grey rabbit thought she heard it saying – *Little rabbit, what's your name? Little rabbit, what's your name?*

"I want my name. I'm going to ask my mother for *my* name!" said the little grey rabbit…

And she turned to run back to her mother at the top of the bank.

But she stopped.

Sharp Nose said, "I can smell the fox…"

Sharp Ears said, "Listen – someone's thumping…"

Sharp Eyes said, "Look – our mother's thumping the ground…"

All four rabbits cried, "It's the *fox*…"

The fox was waiting… between them and their warren.

"*Race* me home..." cried little grey rabbit.
"Run, rabbits, RUN..."
She thumped the ground to give herself
courage – then she ran like the wind!

Her brothers thumped the ground, too, and
raced after little grey rabbit straight towards
the fox!

When she had almost reached him, little grey rabbit darted to one side, then the other. Her brothers also zig-zagged from one side to the other behind her.

The fox lunged after little grey rabbit – but she darted away. He lunged after Sharp Eyes – and *he* changed direction, too.

The fox dashed angrily here and there and suddenly all four little rabbits were safely in the warren, hearts beating wildly.

When she saw that her little rabbits were safe, Mother Rabbit rushed down a hidden hole behind the warren to join them.

"What a great race!" said their mother, proudly.
"Little grey rabbit, your grown-up name is
Racer, and one day…"

But she stopped. Little grey rabbit was fast asleep – and yet her long back feet were twitching. Even in her dreams, Racer was running, ready for whatever adventure might happen next…

Mother rabbit sat down beside the little sleeping rabbit and whispered, "My name is Racer, too."

This way
Little Badger

The day was ending in the big wood.

Someone moved through the trees,
going very slowly…
searching high and low…
Little Badger and his sister, Belle.

Sister Belle knew the big wood well.
But everything was new
to Little Badger,
who had never in his life
been there before.

"Dig, Little Badger,"
said Sister Belle.
"A badger's claws
are made for digging!"

Sister Belle had big, strong
claws, but Little Badger's
claws were small and soft.

The sun went down behind the trees.

"Keep close,"
said Sister Belle.
"The dark is coming."

But, when Sister Belle stopped
to eat a fat white grub,
Little Badger went off on his own
and was soon lost.

Owl swooped down from
the great oak tree and hooted,
"Hurry home, Little Badger!"

"But which way is home?"
cried Little Badger.
"Oh, I wish Sister Belle was
here to show me the way!"

"This way, Little Badger!"
called a voice in the bushes.

Little Badger snuffled deeper
into the wood.

"You're not Sister Belle!"
said Little Badger when he saw…

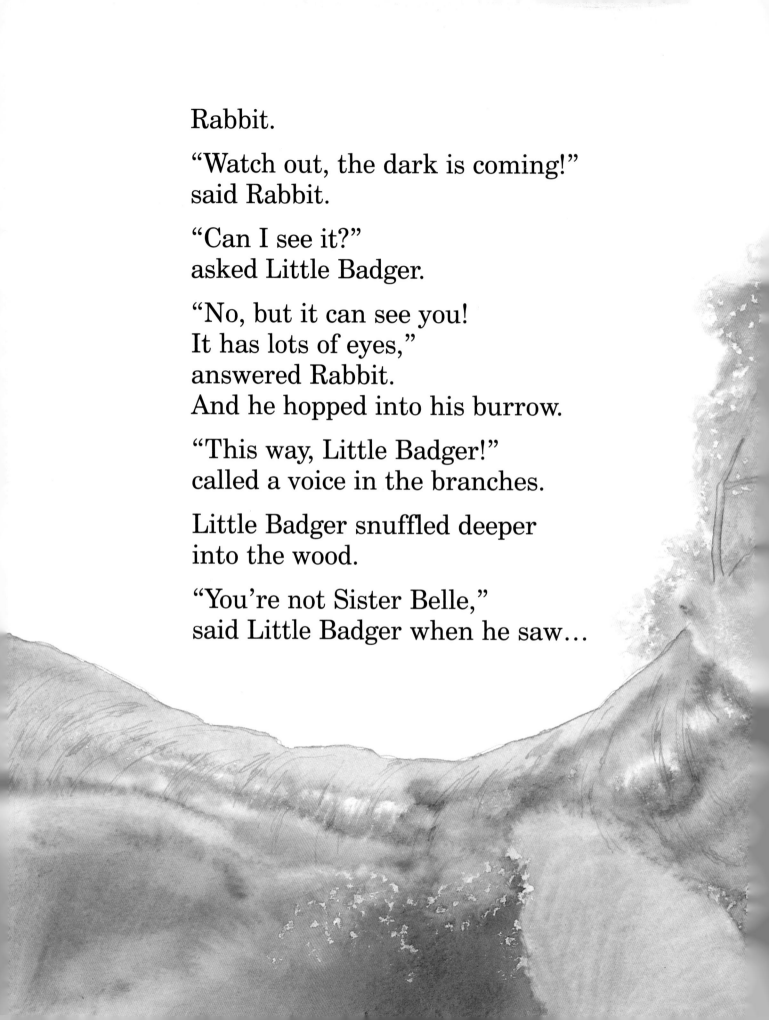

Rabbit.

"Watch out, the dark is coming!"
said Rabbit.

"Can I see it?"
asked Little Badger.

"No, but it can see you!
It has lots of eyes,"
answered Rabbit.
And he hopped into his burrow.

"This way, Little Badger!"
called a voice in the branches.

Little Badger snuffled deeper
into the wood.

"You're not Sister Belle,"
said Little Badger when he saw…

Magpie.

"Watch out, the dark is coming!"
said Magpie.

"Can I talk to it?"
asked Little Badger.

"No, but it can talk to you!
It has lots of voices,"
answered Magpie.
And she flew into her nest.

"This way, Little Badger!"
called a voice in the wet leaves.

Little Badger snuffled deeper
into the wood.

"You're not Sister Belle!"
said Little Badger when he saw…

Mouse.

"Watch out, the dark is coming!"
said Mouse.

"Can I touch it?"
asked Little Badger.

"No, but it can touch you!
It has lots of fingers,"
answered Mouse.
And he ran into his hole.

"What does the dark do when it comes into the wood?" asked Little Badger.

"It chases the daylight away," called Mouse from his hole.

"It fills in the spaces between the branches and the leaves," called Magpie from her nest.

"It makes it hard to see," called Rabbit from his burrow.

"Owl can see!" squeaked Mouse, trembling.

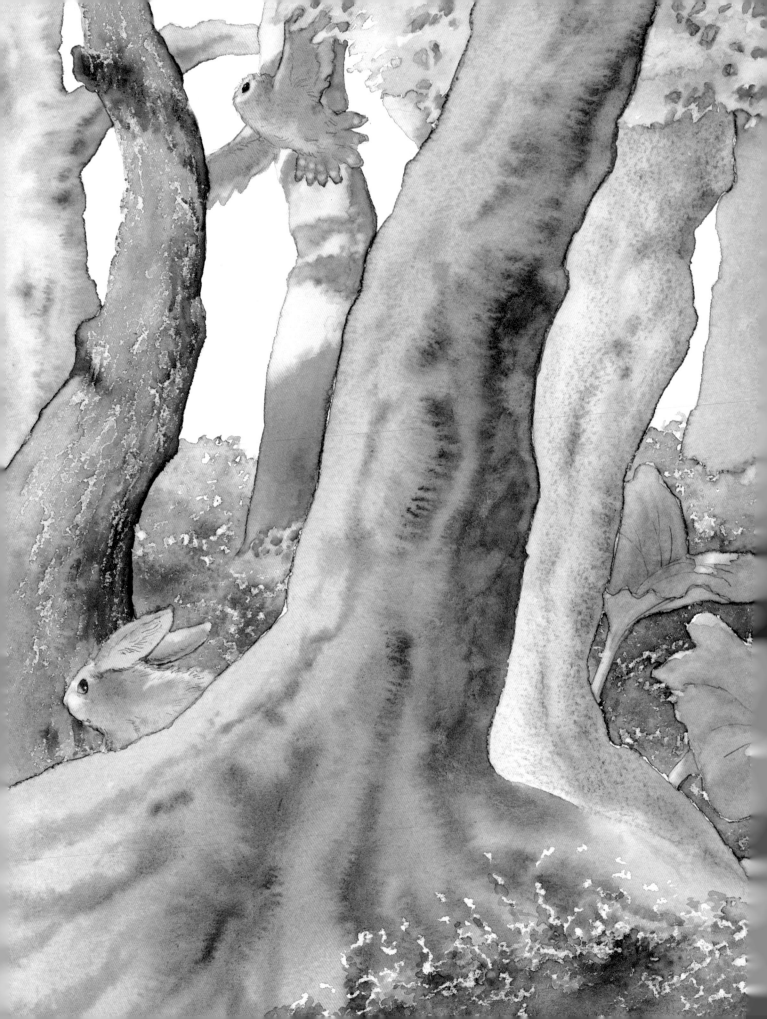

A voice from the edge
of the wood called,
"This way, Little Badger!"

"Is that you, Dark?"
called Little Badger.
But, only an echo answered…
DARK… DARK… DARK!

Owl flew off.
The other animals hid.
And Little Badger…

ran away.

He saw lots of eyes…
and he heard lots of voices.
He felt lots of fingers…
tugging at his fur.

He hid in a deep, inky hole.

Little Badger whispered,
"Are you there, Dark?"

But only an echo answered…
 DARK… DARK… DARK!

He tried to scramble out.
But the walls fell in.
Tree roots and damp earth
covered him from snout to tail.

"Dark has caught me!"
cried Little Badger.

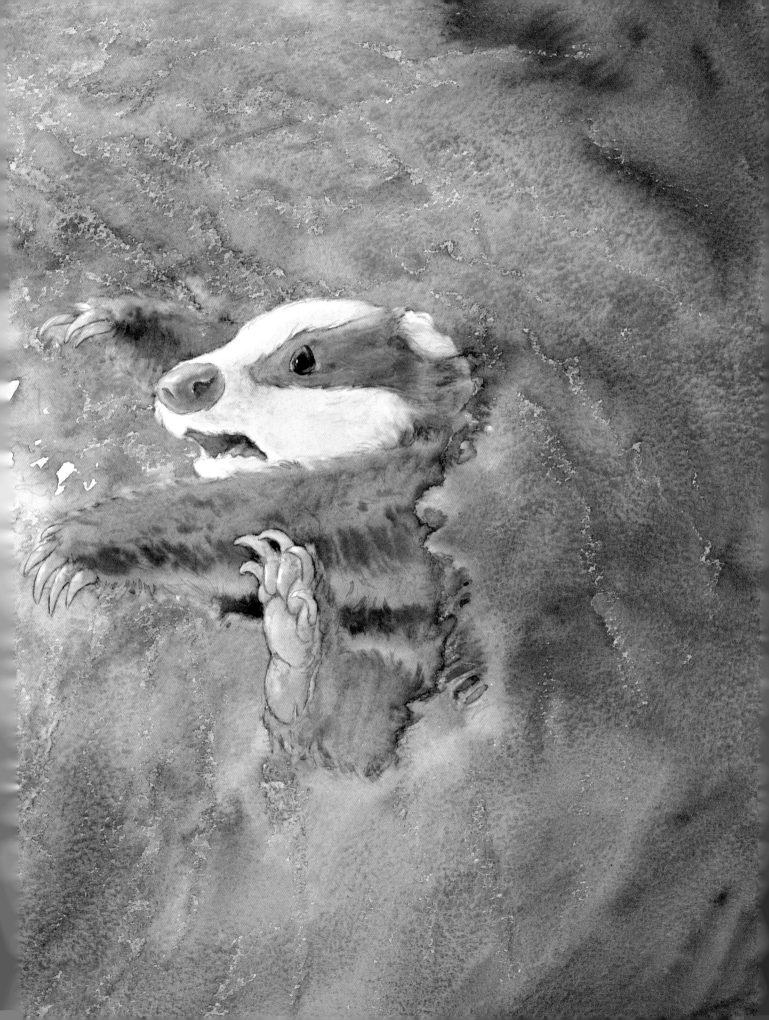

As he lay with the dark all about him,
Little Badger remembered what
Sister Belle had said:
A badger's claws are made for digging!

And Little Badger started to dig...
Dig... Dig... Dig!

And he didn't stop digging until he
was out of that deep, inky hole.

Little Badger shook the dirt out of
his eyes.

Someone moved through the trees,
going very slowly…
searching high and low.
Little Badger saw the moonlight glow.

"Hurrah!" he cried. "It's Sister Belle!"

"Oh, *there* you are, Little Badger,"
cried Sister Belle. "Where have
you been?"

"I couldn't find you, Sister Belle.
Then I got frightened and Dark was
coming," whispered Little Badger.

"You had no need to be afraid,"
smiled Sister Belle. "A badger
learns to like the dark."

"Yes," said Little Badger. "I like it
now. I'll never be afraid again."

The moon came up behind the trees.
The dark went out of the big wood.

Then Sister Belle said,
"This way, Little Badger!"

And she took him home.